WILLIAM SHAKESPEARE'S

Romeo

and

Juliet

**Well-known phrases from Shakespeare's
original work appear in quotes.**

Romeo and Juliet
Re-imagined by Judith Whitmore and Wes Whitmore
Illustrated by Mark Bennett

Published by Smith Terrace Publishing

Illustrations by Mark Bennett
Publishing Consultant, Flying Pig Media
Production & Layout by VMC Art & Design, LLC

ISBN: 978-0-9892157-5-6

William Shakespeare's Romeo and Juliet
Re-imagined by
Judith Whitmore and Wes Whitmore
Illustrated by Mark Bennett

Romeo and Juliet

PROLOGUE

VERONA'S WHERE WE SET OUR STORY
OF RIVAL CLANS, CAPULET AND MONTAGUE,
WHOSE ANCIENT HATE, FIERCE AND GORY,
DEMANDS THAT BLOOD BE SHED ANEW.
EACH CLAN'S LEADER HAS BUT ONE CHILD LEFT,
THEY'LL FORM "A PAIR OF STAR-CROSSED LOVERS"
THEIR MISADVENTURES, AND THEN THEIR DEATH,
BECOME THE GRIEF OUR SAGA COVERS.
THE PARENTS' HATE, IRRATIONAL WRATH,
WHICH ONLY THE TRAGIC DEATHS WILL END,
GIVES WAY TO PEACEFUL AFTERMATH
AND BIDS US LEARN TO NOT OFFEND.

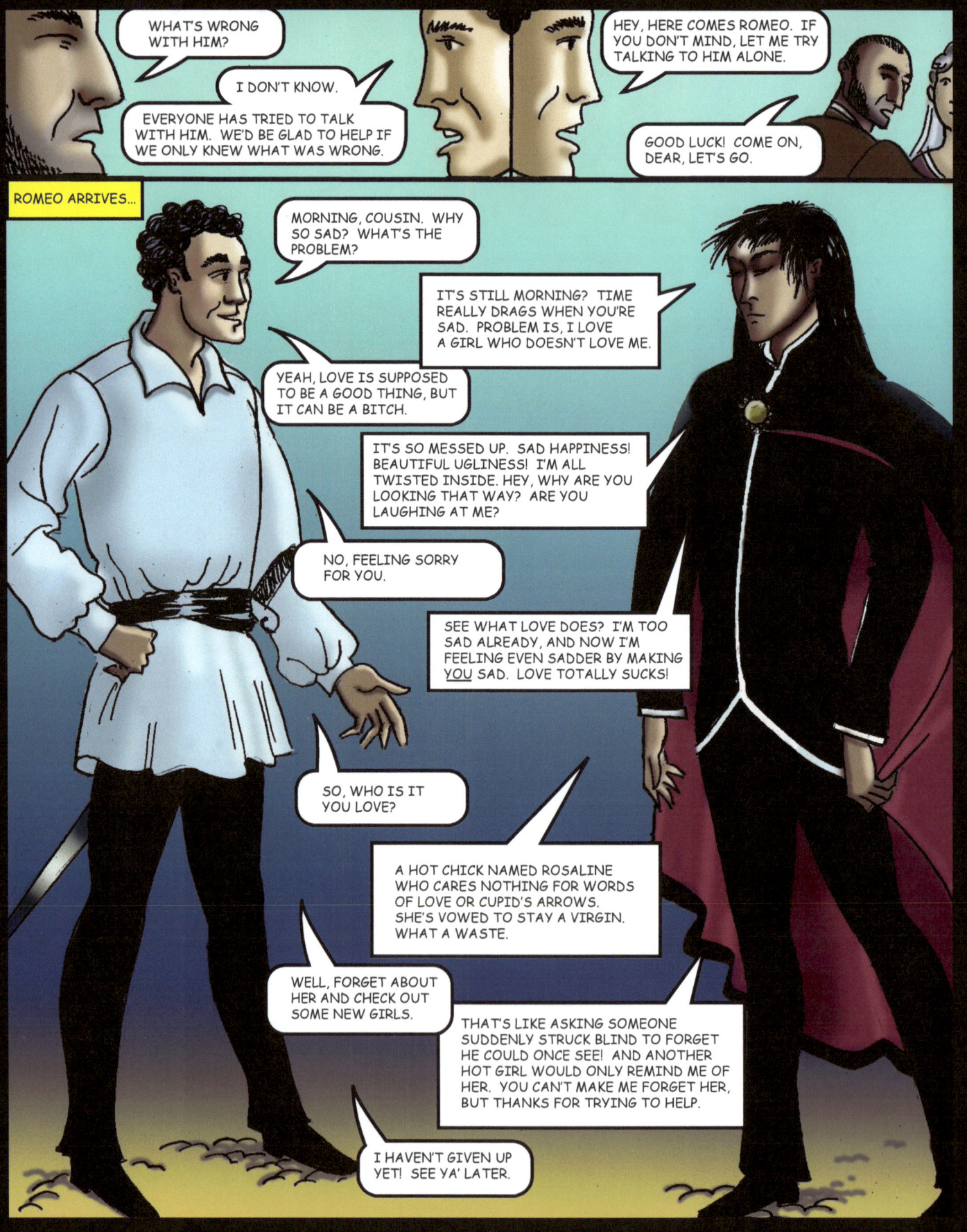

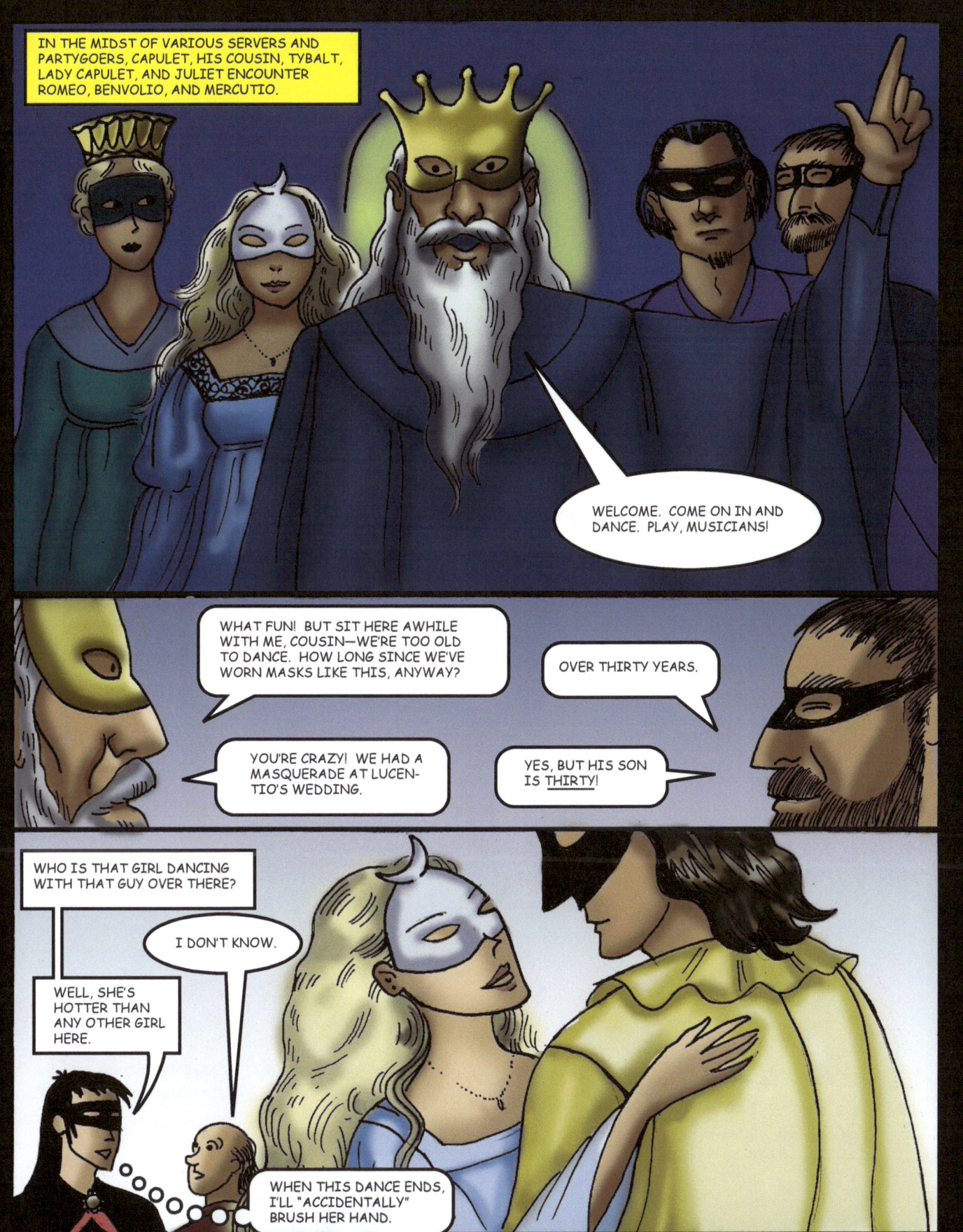

I'LL MAKE SURE SHE'S THERE. I CAN SEE YOU HAVE A GOOD HEART.

WELL, YOU CERTAINLY HAVE A PLAN. MY CONGRATULATIONS AND BLESS YOU BOTH! JULIET DOES SAY THE MOST BEAUTIFUL THINGS ABOUT YOU, BUT I'LL LET HER SPEAK FOR HERSELF THIS AFTERNOON. GOOD LUCK.

WAIT, THERE'S MORE! WHILE WE'RE GETTING MARRIED, ONE OF MY MEN WILL MEET YOU BEHIND THE ABBEY AND GIVE YOU A ROPE LADDER, WHICH I'LL USE TONIGHT TO CLIMB TO MY LOVE'S WINDOW.

WHERE'S NANNY? I SENT HER OVER AN HOUR AGO. GOD, MAYBE SHE CAN'T FIND HIM. NO, THAT'S IMPOSSIBLE, SHE'S JUST OLD AND SLOW. BUT I'M A NERVOUS WRECK.

OH MY GOD, HERE SHE IS. QUICK, NANNY, TELL ME WHAT HE SAID. IS IT BAD NEWS? WHY DO YOU HAVE THAT SAD LOOK ON YOUR FACE?

I'M JUST TIRED FROM WALKING ALL OVER TOWN! LEAVE ME ALONE SO I CAN REST.

ARE YOU KIDDING? I'M GOING MENTAL HERE AND YOU WANT TO REST? HELLO-OH. C'MON, TELL ME WHAT HAPPENED! QUICK!

JEEZ YOU'RE IMPATIENT! OKAY, HERE'S THE DEAL. HURRY OVER TO THE ABBEY WHERE ROMEO'S WAITING TO MAKE YOU HIS WIFE. MEANWHILE, I'LL BE FETCHING A ROPE LADDER WHICH HE'LL USE TO CLIMB TO YOUR BEDROOM WINDOW AFTER DARK TONIGHT. GOOD LORD, YOU'RE BLUSHING!

THANK YOU, NANNY. WISH ME LUCK!

AT THE ABBEY...

MAY GOD BLESS THIS MARRIAGE. I HOPE NOTHING BAD HAPPENS TO MAKE US REGRET IT LATER.

"DITTO" THAT! BUT MISFORTUNE'S NOTHING COMPARED TO THE AWESOME RUSH I GET FROM ONE LOOK AT HER.

BUT LOVE LIKE THIS CAN EXPLODE IN YOUR FACE, LIKE MARRYING FIRE WITH GUNPOWDER. LOVE HER IN MODERATION AND IT WILL LAST.

JULIET ARRIVES

GOOD EVENING, FRIAR. THANKS FOR DOING THIS FOR US.

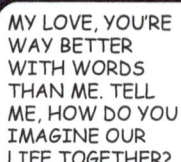

MY LOVE, YOU'RE WAY BETTER WITH WORDS THAN ME. TELL ME, HOW DO YOU IMAGINE OUR LIFE TOGETHER?

INDESCRIBABLE HAPPINESS!

COME, LET'S DO THE JOB. FRANKLY, I DON'T TRUST THE TWO OF YOU ALONE TOGETHER UNTIL YOU'RE MARRIED!

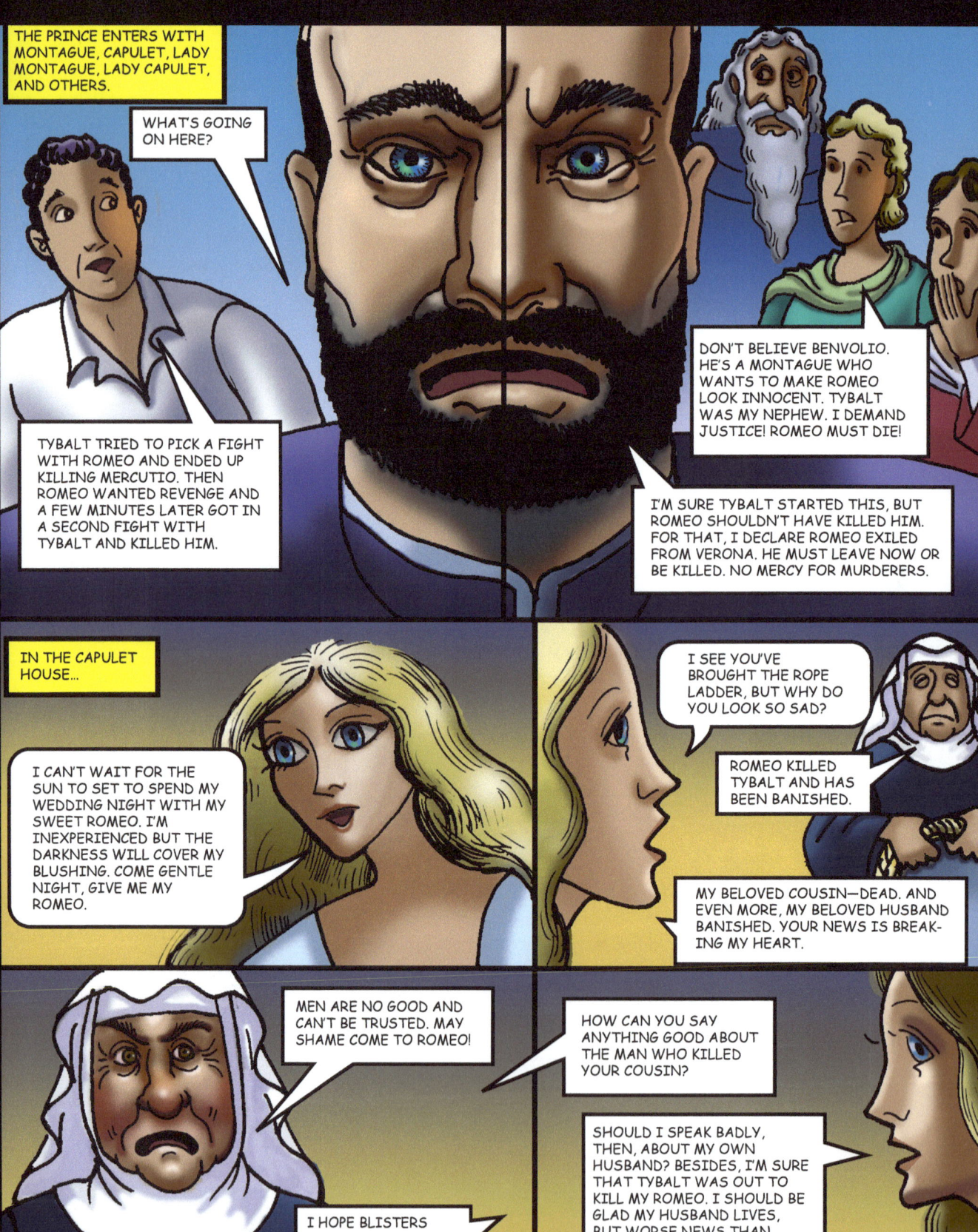

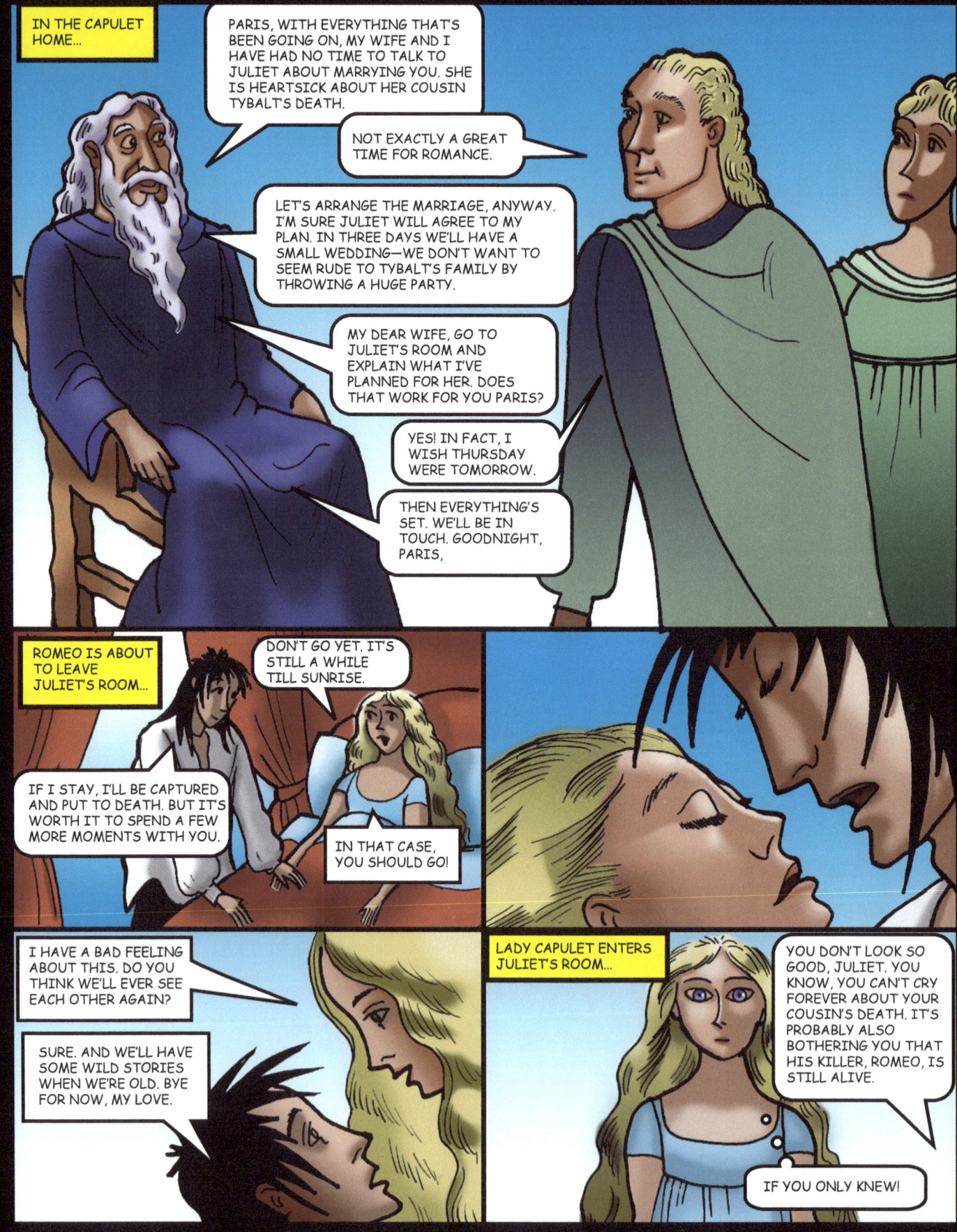

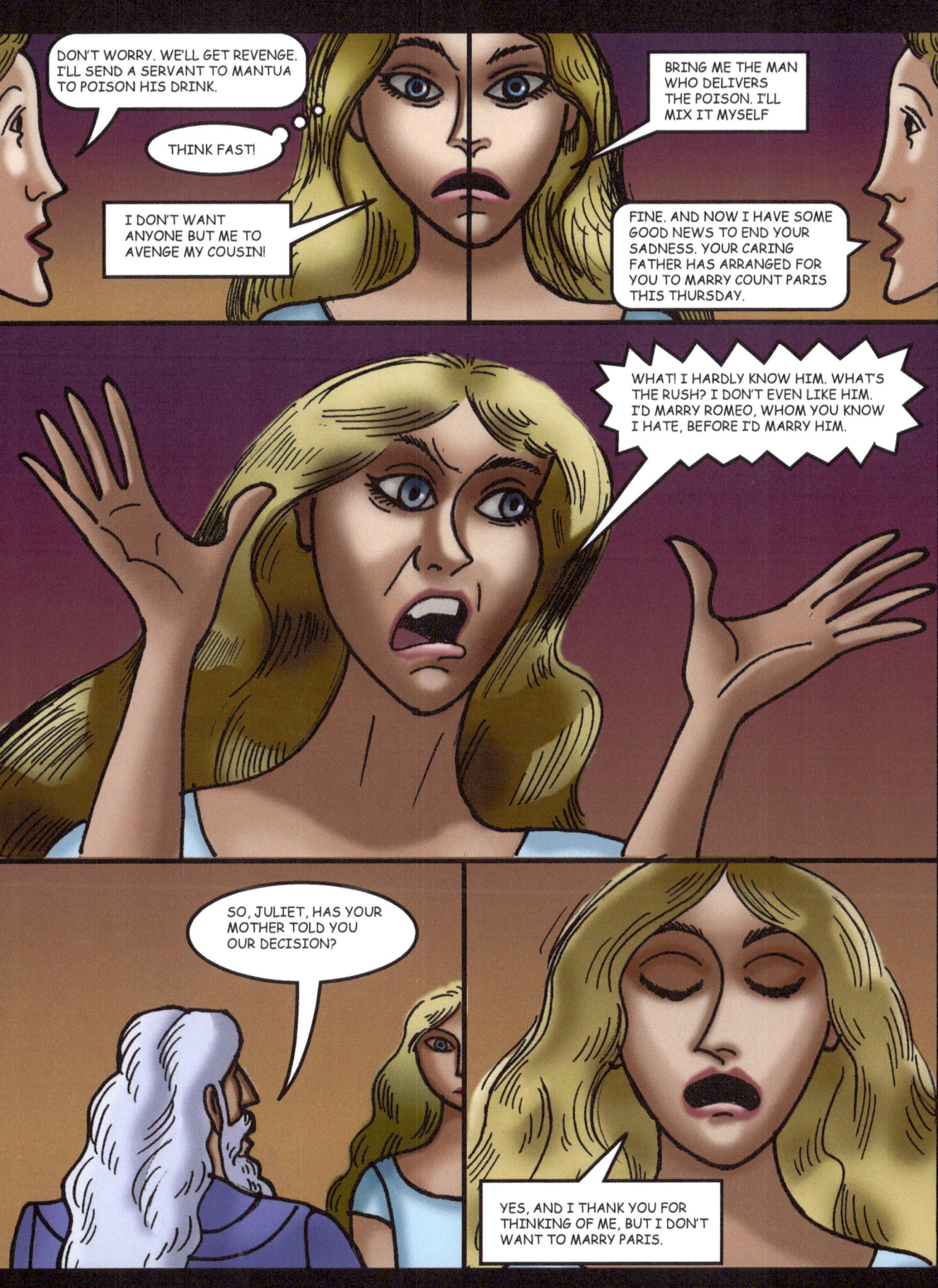

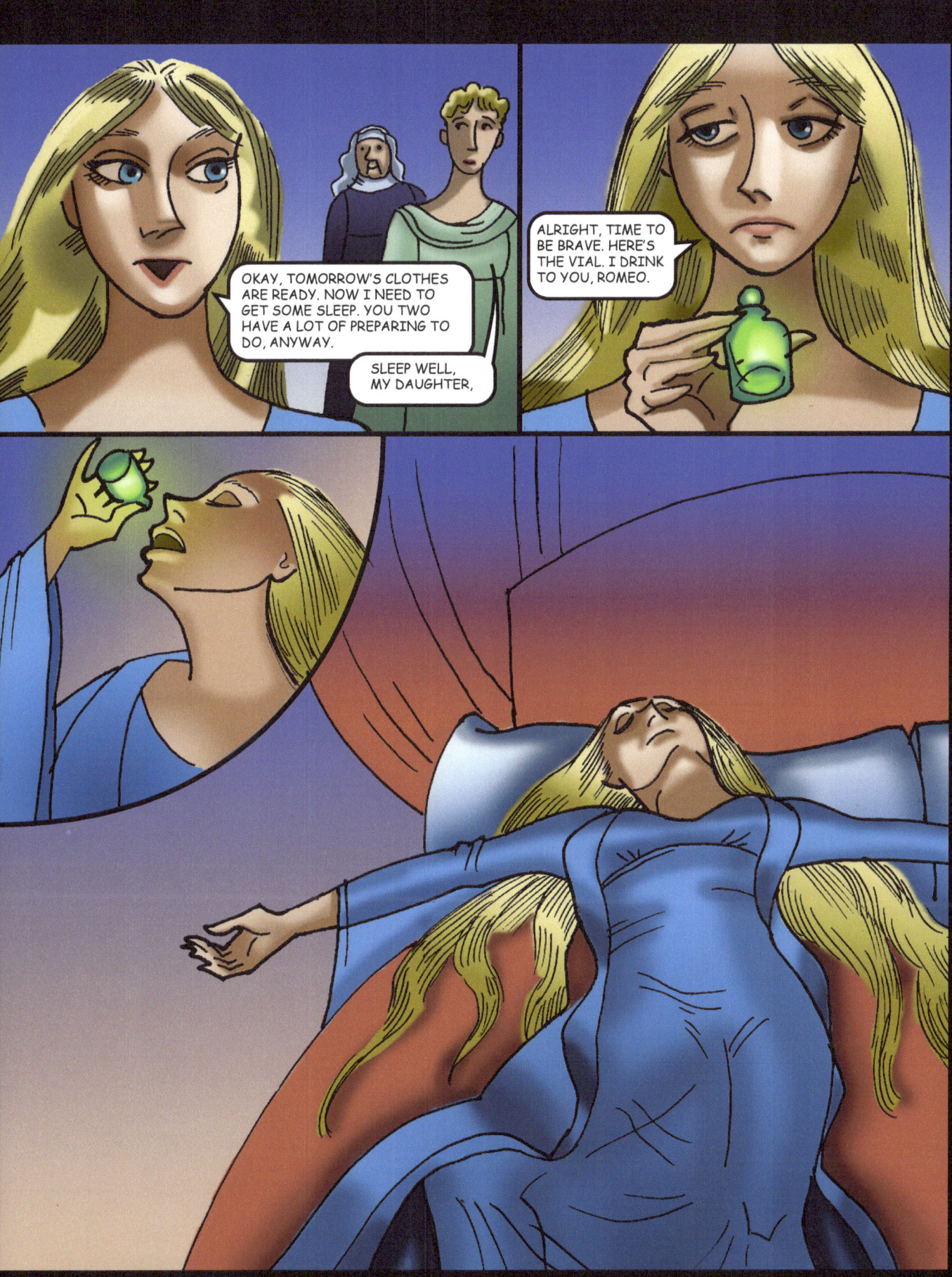

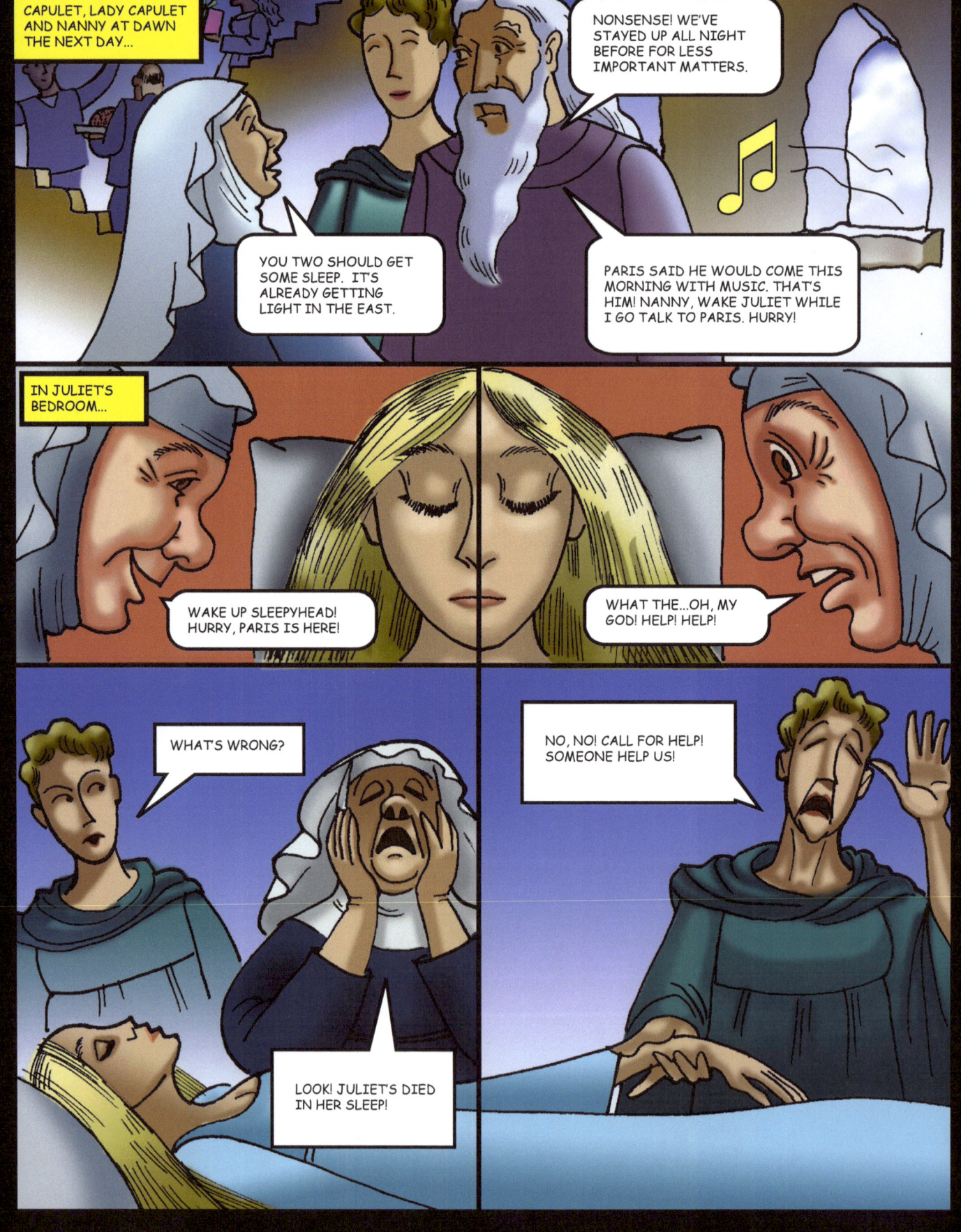

About the Authors

Judith Whitmore is the author of the best-selling romantic-adventure novel *Come Fly with Me* and the cookbook *All Time Favorite Recipes*. In college Judith sang background vocals for Capitol Records, and recently returned to performing with a concert at New York's Carnegie Hall. She has produced theater in Los Angeles and London. Judith has a Master's Degree in Clinical Psychology and is a licensed Marriage and Family Therapist. She is also a licensed commercial pilot, and has flown jets, seaplanes, and hot-air balloons. For eight years, she was a member of Pitkin County Air Rescue and participated in many search and rescue operations.

Wes Whitmore has a Master's Degree in Clinical Psychology and is a licensed Marriage and Family Therapist. He has worked as a volunteer therapist with the Dream Street Foundation at their summer camps for children with life-threatening illnesses. Prior to entering private practice, he traveled worldwide working as a facilitator in human development seminars. Wes enjoys outdoor sports and has been a lifelong surfer and skier.

About the Artist

Mark Bennett is an artist, illustrator and graphic designer. After graduating from Art Center College of Design in Pasadena, he spent 17 years at CBS Television doing artwork and design for The Young and the Restless, The Bold and the Beautiful, The Price is Right and Wheel of Fortune, to name a few. In addition to his freelance commercial work, he continues to produce paintings, prints and ceramics.